Thomas' Travels

Nicolas Starling

London | New York

Published by Clink Street Publishing 2017

Copyright © 2017

First edition.

ISBN:
978-1-911525-92-9 - paperback
978-1-911525-93-6 - ebook

PART ONE

A long time ago when even grandmas and grandads were young, there lived a small creature called a troll. Trolls lived in a country just over the sea from Scotland, a country called Norway. They looked a bit like people but they had long crooked noses and bushy tails. They also had only four fingers on each hand and four toes on each foot. They are friendly but get very angry if tricked. Trolls can only go out at night, because if the sun shines on them they turn to stone.

In Norway there was a very mischievous troll called Thomas. Now Thomas was in all kinds of trouble with the troll elders for being naughty, and he was having to hide all the time because if they caught him they were going to tie the him up in the sun and let him turn to stone. After weeks of hiding and nearly getting caught a few times, Thomas decided that he was going to run away; after all, he was sixty years old and for a troll that is still young. He made plans that he would hide on a sailing ship, and seeing as how trolls could eat and drink anything he would be all right. Thomas packed his clothes and a little bit of money for emergencies, then he told his friend Timothy Troll what he was going to do. Thomas waited for a sailing ship to arrive and after what seemed like weeks, a big ship docked in the harbour where Thomas was hiding. It had three masts and lots of sails and even more rope, which made Thomas very happy because rope was one of his favourite things to eat.

The night before the ship sailed, Thomas sneaked into Troll Town and tricked the troll guard to let him into the town hall. This is where all the troll toffee is kept. Troll toffee is a very special food for trolls, because it makes them very strong and brave. Thomas filled his pockets with toffee and sneaked out before the troll elders caught him. As he was walking down to the sailing ship, all the alarms in Troll Town went off; there were bells and buzzers and bangs. The troll guard had just realised he had been tricked and was very angry. Most of the trolls in Troll Town came out of their houses with their guard dogs, terrier troll dogs, which were very frightening because they didn't bark but roared like a lion. The troll guard was shouting, 'ALL THE TROLL TOFFEE HAS BEEN STOLEN BY THOMAS, WE MUST STOP HIM QUICKLY!'

When Thomas heard all the trolls shouting and the dogs roaring he said to himself *ooh 'eck, I had better run*. Now Thomas wasn't very big – after all, he was only sixty – and he could run like the wind and was very good at hiding. He could hear all the trolls and dogs of Troll Town getting nearer and nearer, so he started running as fast as he could down the hill to the ship. As he ran, he was that busy thinking about escaping that he tripped over his tail. When trolls do that, which they all do from time to time, they roll up like a ball and stop eventually, but when Thomas did this he was going down to the sea and couldn't stop, so he just closed his eyes and hoped the water wasn't too cold.

He hit the water with such a splash that the dogs heard him and they let out a mighty, 'ROAR!' then started to run down the hill to the sea. As he heard them coming, he swam to the anchor chain, which was good because only having four fingers and four toes on each limb, trolls find it hard to swim. Thomas thought, *what shall I do now? I know!* and he went underwater so just the tip of his crooked nose was sticking out for him to breath. Then he grabbed hold of the anchor chain with his hands and feet and wrapped his tail round for extra grip and waited. As he waited, he thought, *how am I going to get out of this? I have made all the trolls of Troll Town angry because I tricked them.*

The water of Norway is very clean and clear and Thomas could see all the trolls and dogs looking for him, and just to make things worse, Thomas saw three ticklefish swimming towards him. Ticklefish are very special they can breathe in or out of water and have long soft fins that tickle anything they touch. They also use their fins to fly like a bird and go anywhere they want, but are very hard to see unless you are a troll.

As Thomas held the anchor chain, the ticklefish got closer and closer, but Thomas daren't move in case they saw him. They swam all round Thomas and still he didn't move, until one of them swam into his furry tail and the other two waited until it came out. Then they swam really close to Thomas's tail with their soft fins. Thomas watched the fish and giggled and small bubbles came out of his mouth, but he didn't mind because he realised the fish that swam into his tail was a mummy fish and she had laid some eggs in his tail; the other two fanned them right in to make sure they are safe. But then mummy fish swam up to Thomas's face and tickled him under his crooked nose, which made him sneeze, and when trolls sneeze underwater they make more bubbles than a bubble bath and a very loud splash.

When all the bubbles had popped, Thomas looked up through the water and saw all the angry trolls of Troll Town looking at him and shaking their fists and two of the troll elders were there, looking down at him. 'You are a very lucky troll,' they said, 'it will be daybreak shortly and we have to go home before the sun comes out or we will turn to stone. But we will come back later to get you.'

As soon as they had gone, Thomas climbed up the anchor chain and into the ship; the part where they keep the chain when they are at sea. Thomas was wet, cold and tired, and the room he was in was warm and dark so he crawled under a piece of old sail and went to sleep.

When Thomas woke up he was very hungry, so he peeped out of the hole where the anchor goes and it was dark. Then he felt the ship moving and in the distance, saw tiny lights flickering; he realised they were at sea and the tiny lights were Troll Town. Thomas jumped for joy and thought *hurray, I've escaped the troll elders*. He danced around the room singing and shouting at the top of his voice, but then he heard a loud booming voice.

'AVAST, ME HEARTIES, WHO'S MAKING ALL THAT NOISE?'

'I don't know captain, it's none of us,' said a sailor.

'If it's not you and it's not me,' said the captain, 'then we must have a stowaway. The man who finds him gets extra pirate pop.'

When Thomas heard the captain, he hid in the anchor chain and curled himself up as small as he could and listened to all the sailors looking for him. He heard one of the sailors say, 'I hope I find the stowaway because Captain Jellybelly is very good with his rewards.'

Captain Jellybelly was one of the nicest pirate captains there was, but he ate all day and had a huge belly that shook like jelly. His favourite things were cakes ice cream biscuits and sweets so he didn't like stowaways because they had to be fed.

As the sailors looked for Thomas, he thought to himself, *why am I always hiding from people? This time I am going to be brave.* He took some troll toffee out of his pocket, broke a small piece off and ate it. After a few minutes he could feel his muscles getting bigger and bigger, and he felt as brave as brave could be. He felt so brave he climbed out of the anchor chain and shouted, 'I AM HERE YOU LILY-LIVERED PIRATE. COME AND GET ME IF YOU DARE.'

There was a loud growl and a pirate burst through the door with his sword in his hand, but he stopped dead In his tracks when he saw Thomas. His eyes widened and his mouth fell open, and he laughed so much tears rolled down his cheeks.

'How dare you laugh at me?' shouted Thomas. 'I am Thomas the mighty troll and what I lack in height I make up in strength and bravery.'

The pirate laughed even more. He laughed so much he was helpless, and this made Thomas very angry – so angry that he ran up to the pirate and kicked him on the shin as hard as he could. The pirate let go of his sword and rubbed his shin with both hands. Thomas picked up the sword, which was as light as a feather to him because he had eaten some troll toffee, and he ran behind the pirate and jabbed him up the backside. The pirate squealed, jumped in the air and banged his head on the roof, which made him very dizzy. As he was sat on the floor with his head spinning, Thomas said to him, 'That will teach you to laugh at me, Thomas the mighty troll. Now stand up and take me to your captain and tell him what I did to you, or else you will be in serious trouble.'

The pirate took Thomas to Captain Jellybelly and said, 'I have found the stowaway, Captain. He is called Thomas the mighty troll. Be careful, Captain, he is as strong as twenty pirates and as brave as a giant even though he is only small.'

Captain Jellybelly bent down and said to Thomas, 'Is this true, little troll?'

Then he picked up Thomas by his tail and said, 'Can you prove how brave and strong you are before I eat you for my supper?'

Thomas suddenly remembered the ticklefish eggs in his furry tail and thought Captain Jellybelly might squash them, so he reached out, grabbed the captain's beard and pulled a big piece of it out.

Captain Jellybelly let out a very loud yelp, let go of Thomas and fell on his very large belly and couldn't get up again. He just rocked back and forth like a rocking horse. Thomas marched over to him and said, 'Was that brave enough and strong enough for you?'

As the captain struggled to stand up, Thomas said to him, 'I would like to become a pirate on your ship. I would like to be your friend and I would be the night watchman and keep you all safe while you are asleep.'

The captain looked at Thomas and thought, *somebody so brave and strong would be good to have as a friend and with him being so little he can't eat that much.* So he said, 'OK, you can be watchman on my ship *The Naughty Elf.* They say there are elves on board, so be careful; if you crash or sink her I will feed you to the fish.'

So Thomas went to his cabin while it was still dark. He was so hungry he ate three inches of rope, had a cup of pirate pop then he thought that he had better check the ticklefish eggs. Thomas looked carefully at each egg and they were all fine, but he thought it would be better if he took them out of the fur in his tail and put them somewhere warm and safe. He decided that the best place would be the piece of Captain Jellybelly's beard that he had pulled out. So Thomas sneaked out quickly before it got light, picked up the beard and took it to his cabin. Then he took the eggs out of the fur on his tail, one by one, and looked at them closely. He noticed there were different kinds of eggs and that meant only one thing. A lot of the eggs will be invisible ticklefish. These are very naughty cheeky fish that do things like

11

hide in mummy and daddy's hands, and tickle children on their tummies, feet, or wherever makes them laugh. Thomas put all the eggs gently into the bit of beard and hid it safely, then he promised himself that he would look after the ticklefish because it was good fun when they made mums and dads tickle children. Then he made himself a hammock and had a nap till teatime.

He woke up happy after his nap he had been dreaming about the ticklefish being naughty and he hoped he would see them do it again one day. He had his tea and said to himself, 'Ah well, I had better go to work. I don't want to be late on my first day as a pirate.'

Thomas went to the captain and said, 'Pirate Tom reporting for duty, Captain,' and Captain Jellybelly said, 'Right, if you climb the main mast to the crow's nest and keep watch for any ship that passes, or any land, you must shout and tell me because we are getting short of food; we only have thirty trifles and twenty packets of biscuits left, which might last me two days.'

As Thomas was climbing up the mast he thought to himself, *this is a long way for me to climb with my little legs. I will be tired by the time I get to the top. I might have a little sleep, no one will know.* When Thomas finally got up to the crow's nest, he was very tired. His legs ached and there was a strange fly with bright green wings buzzing round his head and it kept landing on his shoulder. The noise it made was a quiet, squeaky noise; it was like nothing he had heard before. Thomas thought, *if I leave it alone it might go away so I will have a rest and ignore it.* The next thing Thomas knew, something was pulling his hair and making a noise. He opened his eyes and saw the fly with green wings had arms and legs, so Thomas stood up to catch it but as he looked out of the crow's nest, he saw a sailing ship that had lots of lights and music and people dancing. Thomas knew straight away that it was a holiday ship, a cruise liner.

Thomas shouted down to the captain ship, 'Ahoy, on the left hand side.' Then he thought to himself, *I am going to have to learn which side is port and which side is starboard*. Then Thomas looked for the fly, but could not see him anywhere so he watched all the pirates starting their work.

The captain was shouting, 'LOAD THE SLIME CANNON. FILL THE WATER PISTOLS . GET THE STINK BOMB GRENADES,' as he steered the *Naughty Elf* towards the cruise ship. When they were nearly touching the cruise ship, the captain said, 'FIRE THE CANNON,' so the pirates popped a big balloon at the back of the cannon and all the air rushed up the barrel of the cannon and fired slime all over the people on the cruise ship. It dripped off the people and onto the floor, making everybody slip and slide and fall over.

The captain said, 'Right lads, let's board the cruise ship.'

They all jumped onto the cruise ship, squirting all the slime out of way with their water pistols. Then two of the pirates ran down to the kitchen and threw three stink bombs in. They didn't have to wait long before all people who worked in the kitchen ran out holding their noses. The pirates put hankies over their noses and ran into the kitchen, which was full of all kinds of lovely food.

One of the pirates said, 'Come and help us collect the food, there's too much for us to carry.'

Six more pirates ran to the kitchen, picked up any food they could and carried it back to their own ship. It took about thirty minutes to fill the kitchen on the *Naughty Elf* and there was only food like cabbage and turnip and liver left. So Captain Jellybelly said to the people on the cruise ship he would leave that food for them.

When Captain Jellybelly had let the other ship go, he and his crew sat down and had a really good feed. The captain ate four trifles, six cream cakes and four packets of chocolate biscuits, then he drank two big bottles of pirate pop. While they were eating the Captain stood up and said to the pirates, 'A big hurray to Thomas for spotting such a big ship full of food.'

Thomas blushed and said it was easy, but he didn't dare tell them it was the funny fly with the green wings that had woken him. All the pirates cheered Thomas ,and he asked if he could go to his cabin because he had been up all night.

The first thing Thomas did when he got to his cabin was check the ticklefish eggs and make sure they were all right. He checked each egg and saw that they were getting bigger and looked healthy, so he tucked them up in the beard and put them back in the hiding place.

Thomas was just going to have his sleep and was just taking his clothes off when he smelt under his arms. *Phew! I STINK*, he said to himself, *I had better have a bath.* So he sat on his hammock and started thinking what he could use for a bath. As he was thinking, the little green winged fly flew into his cabin and buzzed around.

Thomas tried to catch it but it was too quick for him, so he said, 'Don't worry, fly, I will not hurt you because you woke me up so we could catch the ship and get some food. As a matter of fact, if it is possible, I would like to be your friend because it can get very lonely being a pirate.'

The little fly flew to a corner of the room and with a flash of glittering cloud the fly changed into a magic elf. 'Hello, my name is Ronnie Elf. I was trying to talk to you earlier but I had to be quiet as you are the only one that knows I'm here. You are right about it being lonely but I think the other pirates are much too rough for me, I am a little bit frightened of them so I stay small when they are about.'

'Well,' said Thomas, 'I promise that I will not tell anybody about you and we can be friends and meet in the crow's nest at night and keep each other company, but please tell me a little bit about yourself now.'

The two of them talked for hours. Thomas told Ronnie all about the trouble he was in in Norway and about how he couldn't go out in the sunshine. He also told him about the troll toffee and the ticklefish.

Then Ronnie said, 'I know all about you. Elves are nosy creatures that must find out all they can; we are also magic and mischievous like trolls, that is why I decided to let you know I was here. I think we could have some good fun.'

Thomas looked out of the window and it was just about dark. 'Oh no,' he said to Ronnie, 'I have to go to work again and I haven't had a sleep yet.'

'Don't worry,' said Ronnie, 'now we are friends we will help each other.'

So Thomas climbed the mast to the crow's nest, then fell into a big heap, he was that tired. Ronnie said to him, 'You have a sleep and I will be lookout for a while. Oh, and by the way, you do need a bath.'

Thomas just lay where he was, said thank you to Ronnie, and went to sleep.

**

When Thomas woke up, he looked for Ronnie and saw he had turned back into a fly. He said, 'Is everything all right, Ronnie?'

Ronnie answered that everything was fine and it was his turn to be lookout. Thomas took over and Ronnie said he just had some things to do and a little nap, then he would be back before daylight. After he had gone Thomas thought to himself how lucky he was to have found a friend like Ronnie and he just stood daydreaming and looking at the stars.

Before he knew it Ronnie was back and it was nearly daylight. Thomas was very frightened about turning into stone and said quickly, 'I have to get out of the sun.'

Ronnie said, 'Don't worry, Thomas, I have made a spell for you so you can go out in the daylight.' Then Ronnie made Thomas stand still and cast the spell.

'Hubble, bubble, toil and trouble. Protect poor Thomas with a blackness bubble.'

Thomas said, 'Will that protect me really, or are you just being naughty?'

Ronnie answered him, 'I promise it will protect you, and when you have that bath it will disappear from sight but stay with you forever. The only thing you must not do is get water from Norway on it.'

Thomas said that as they were friends, he trusted him, and would try it out today so long as he was around with a spell just in case it didn't work. They both went to Thomas's cabin and when they got there and went in there was a little bucket of nice warm water and some soap.

Ronnie said, 'I am really glad we are friends and hopefully one day we will be best friends but not when you smell like that. So I have magicked you a warm bath that never goes cold and never runs out, I don't think you know but ticklefish eggs love a wash as well so they will be able to use it.'

Thomas undressed and got in the nice warm bath. He was so happy and comfy and warm. He said to Ronnie, 'Thank you so much for everything you have done for me. I think you are the nicest elf there is, all though you are the only one I have met. I will help you any way I can, and I think we should be best friends. I will even make sure I carry troll toffee in case we get in trouble.'

'Well,' said Ronnie, 'I have never had a best friend before and it sounds really good. We can get up to all sorts of mischief, but first of all we must try the blackness bubble to see if it works, so get out of the bath. You have been in there long enough anyway.'

All of a sudden, Thomas felt nervous about going out in the sun. He had seen hundreds of trolls that had turned to stone because they got caught in the sun. And what made matters worse is that humans used them as ornaments, doorsteps and things like that.

'You did say you will be with me in case it doesn't work?' asked Thomas.

'Yes I did,' answered Ronnie, 'but I will have to turn into a fly because the pirates don't know I'm on board and we must not tell them.'

So Thomas got out of the bath and the blackness bubble had shrunk round his body and turned invisible, so he went to his cabin door and put his leg out and it didn't turn to stone, so he tried his hand and that was all right; so he took a deep breath, closed his eyes, and walked out into the sunshine

He stood there and for the first time he felt the sun on him and how nice and warm it is. He would have stayed there forever, but Ronnie said to him, 'Come on, Thomas, stop day dreaming, we have got the ticklefish to bathe.'

They went down to the cabin and took the ticklefish out of their hiding place and looked at them all before they put them in the bath, then they both sat down and watched them while they talked about the fun they would have.

As they were talking, they heard Captain Jellybelly shout, 'MAN THE SLIME CANNONS, LOAD THE WATER PISTOLS, WE ARE ABOUT TO BE ATTACKED BY CAPTAIN WILLY WELK!'

Willy Welk was the oldest, most grizzly captain in the English navy and he had sneaked up on Captain Jellybelly. 'Oh no,' said Thomas, 'Now we are in trouble, we will have to fight the navy, and I don't like fighting, it's so messy.'

But the captain shouted for all the pirates to go on deck, so Thomas was about to leave his cabin when Ronnie said, 'Have some troll toffee and I will help if I can,' then he changed into a fly and flew out of the window.

Thomas quickly ate a piece of toffee and before he had got onto the deck of the ship, he felt as strong as a horse and brave as brave can be. He looked at Captain Jellybelly and the captain said, 'Get yourself a water pistol, Thomas, and fill it full of rose water; that smells nice, and English sailors don't like to smell like that.' Then Captain Jellybelly said to the pirates, 'Fire when you can see the custard drips on their shirts.'

Thomas, feeling so strong and brave, saw the custard drips first and fired his water pistol that was full of nice-smelling rose water, and the sailor cried out, 'Oh no, Captain, they are shooting us with perfume and it's 'orrible.'

'Did they?' said the captain. 'If they want to fight dirty, we will show them. MAN THE CANDYFLOSS CANNONS.'

Then the battle started.

Candyfloss cannons were fired, making it very sticky for the pirates to move and poor Ronnie, who had changed into a fly, was stuck to the floor. The pirates fired their slime cannons and the sailors were skidding all over. Then the pirates squirted them with rose water, which made Captain Welk very angry, and he shouted, 'LOAD the big cannon with tapioca, that should stop them.'

Just before they fired the big tapioca cannon, Thomas saw Ronnie stuck to the floor with candyfloss and dashed over to help him get free. 'Quickly,' shouted Thomas, 'we must get you free before they fire the cannon.'

Thomas bent down and with troll toffee speed, he ate all the candyfloss round Ronnie and freed him. 'Quickly fly up to the crow's nest, you will be safe there,' said Thomas.

Ronnie had just got to the crow's nest and there was a bang like thunder; it was the big cannon being fired. Tapioca fell out of the sky like frogs spawn covering all the naughty elf and the pirates and Captain Jellybelly. Jellybelly didn't know what to do. He realised that Captain Welk had better weapons than him and that he had lost the battle, so he said to the pirates, 'Haul the mainsail,' but he was too late: Captain Welk and the sailors had captured the *Naughty Elf* and the pirates.

The sailors locked the pirates in the ship's dungeons, but they didn't see Thomas. With him being small, he could easily hide, so he waited until everybody was hard at work cleaning the *Naughty Elf* and he sneaked down to his cabin. Ronnie was already there and he was shaking with fright. He didn't know what he would do if he got caught. He rushed over to Thomas and gave him a big cuddle and said, 'Thank you, thank you for saving me, I was ever so frightened. I could have been caught or worse, I could have been squashed.'

'It's all right, don't worry, you looked after me earlier, that's what friends do. Let's go and have a look at the ticklefish and make sure they are all right, then we can have some tapioca candyfloss and some pirate pop and talk about how we are going to escape, because I have had enough of being a pirate.'

When they looked in the bath they saw that the ticklefish had hatched. There were hundreds of tiny fish swimming in the bath; every one had a smile on its face. Invisible ticklefish really were invisible, and all you could see was a trail of bubbles where they had been.

'Have you any idea what to feed them on to make them grow bigger?' Thomas asked Ronnie.

'I think they like bread and cakes and cabbage,' Ronnie answered. 'When it's dark, I will fly down to the kitchen to see if I can get anything, but until then I think we should relax and have a nap.'

***

After their nap the two of them sat on the floor of the cabin, ate some more tapioca and drank more pirate pop. Then they talked about how to get off the ship.

'We could help Captain Jellybelly escape. I have heard Captain Willy Welk is going to send them all to a school for naughty pirates to teach them some manners and how to behave. I don't think they would like that, so we could tell Jellybelly we want to be let off the ship in the country they call England.'

'Well, we are near England,' said Ronnie. 'You can see it if you look out of the window. We could swim, it would be better for us.'

'You know the pirates frighten me and I don't trust them, Ronnie.'

'Or we could stay on board Captain Welks' ship and sneak off in England, and that would give us more time to look after the ticklefish and they will be big enough to look after themselves.'

They decided they had better see if they could get some food, and Ronnie flew down to the kitchen and came back with an armful of food. When they had fed the ticklefish, they talked some more about how they were going to escape and Ronnie said he thought they should stay here because there was loads of lovely food on board, and it was warm and dry.

Thomas agreed with him because he wasn't very good at swimming. 'And also,' he said, 'We will not have to work because nobody knows we are here.'

They spent the next few days eating sleeping and playing tricks on the sailors like tying their shoelaces together and when they walked they fell over, and putting salt in their pirate pop. But best of all, they waited till the sailors were all asleep, making scary noises and frightening them.

One morning, they had just got up and were feeding the ticklefish – which were big enough to look after themselves, but Thomas and Ronnie liked to spoil them – when they heard Captain Welk shout, 'All hands on deck, we are just about to dock in London.'

Thomas and Ronnie got very excited. They had never been to England before, and they were going to start their new adventure in the capital.

'Quickly,' said Ronnie, 'Pack your things, and don't forget your troll toffee, you might need it.'

After they had packed everything they needed, they looked out of the window and saw that they had docked in the middle of London and all the sailors were busy putting the sails and ropes away.

Ronnie said, 'Just one thing to do before we start our new adventure and that is to let the ticklefish go.' So they carefully picked up the bath and said, 'Bye bye, ticklefish, I hope you have fun,' then tipped them in the water.

Both Thomas and Ronnie giggled at the thought that shortly ticklefish would be everywhere in England making grown-ups, especially mummies and daddies, tickle little boys and girls.

When the fish had gone, Thomas and Ronnie sneaked off the boat and saw a very stern looking headmaster waiting for Captain Jellybelly and the pirates. They both laughed and said, 'I bet they're in trouble!'

They went over to the headmaster and blew him a raspberry, then they ran away laughing. 'Well, Thomas, I think our first job will be to find somewhere warm and dry to live and then we can explore and have some fun. I have heard they have a thing called a zoo in England, it's where lost and orphaned animals go I think. Shall we see if London has one? I think they will be warm and dry, with lots of food.'

'That is an awesome idea,' said Thomas, 'let's go and see if we can find it.'

So off they went up and down streets looking for the zoo, but couldn't find anything.

'We shall have to learn to read English if we are going to live here,' Ronnie told Thomas.

'Yes, but where do you start? They use funny letters here.'

'I know,' said Ronnie, 'you go and hide in that bush and I will magic into a human and go see if I can find out anything.'

While Ronnie was trying to find out if there was a zoo and find out about learning to read, Thomas made himself comfortable in the bush. He looked around him and saw all kinds of rubbish and food on the floor, so he made himself a place to lay down and picked up a piece of fruit he thought it was an apple core and had a little bit. It was lovely, so he lay there, warm, comfy and dry, and thought to himself, *Humans are messy, they just throw things on the floor instead of using rubbish bins. But it does mean that we will not go hungry.*

As Thomas lay under the bush waiting out of the corner of his eye, he saw something move; it made him jump, so he just laid still and didn't move as he watched a beautifully red robin hop right up to him and share his apple core. Thomas quietly said hello to the robin and gently stroked his feathers; the robin chirped at him then joyfully sang his song. He decided then that he had so much to learn in England, and he thought he would have fun doing it.

Just as he was watching the robin, Ronnie arrived. He had changed back to a fly and flew into the bush, and when the robin saw him, it tried to eat him for a snack. Ronnie thought quickly and hissed at him like an angry cat, which made the robin fly off. 'Phew,' he said, 'that was close. I hope it's not going to be like that all the time.

'Anyway, I have found out there is a zoo in London and I know where it is. Unfortunately it's too far for us to walk in one go, and I have used too much magic for now so we will have to find somewhere to sleep, somewhere without the chance of me been eaten.'

The two ran from bush to bush looking for a safe place to spend the night, when eventually they heard two people saying, 'Shall we go to the fish and chip shop for our supper before it closes?' As they began walking, Thomas and Ronnie followed them secretly without being seen. Then, when they got there, they heard the man that worked there say, 'You have only just made it, we are about to close.'

The people got their supper, and as they opened the door to get out, Ronnie flew in, but Thomas didn't manage to run in and the man came from the back of the counter and locked the door. So Thomas was on the outside and Ronnie was locked inside.

They waited until the man had tidied everything up and was just going home when he saw Ronnie and thought he was a fly. He went back round the counter and picked up a fly swat and hit Ronnie with it; he hit him that hard that he crashed against the wall and knocked himself out.

When the man finally left, Thomas tried to climb up to the letter box in the bottom of the door, but he wasn'tbig enough to reach. So he had a little piece of troll toffee, waited a minute for it to work, and jumped up to the letterbox, pushed it open and jumped down to the floor easily. Then he ran over to Ronnie, who was awake but still dizzy.

'You sit there,' Thomas said. 'I will sort everything out and make it comfy and safe for us.' Then he ran round to the back of the counter to look for things. The first thing he found was a bottle of milk that had been opened, so he got an empty carton that you put fish and chips in, then he found a little plastic spoon that you use to eat mushy peas with. He poured some milk into the fish and chip carton and picked it all up with no problem, and took it all to Ronnie, who was still sat on the floor.

Ronnie looked up and said, 'How did you carry all that?'

Thomas replied, 'It's easy if you have troll toffee first,' then he helped Ronnie stand up and he took him over to the carton where they both drank all the milk. Then both of them climbed into the carton and pulled the lid on. They snuggled down and were warm and comfy; they both fell asleep feeling happy and safe.

They woke up early in the morning and Thomas asked Ronnie if he felt better. Ronnie said he did, but he would have to be careful. They had only been in England one night and a bird had tried to eat him and a man had bashed him with a fly swat. 'Anyway,' he said, 'We had better leave before the man comes back to work.' So Ronnie flew onto the letterbox ledge and reached down to help Thomas climb up; that way it would save the toffee.

Thomas had tucked the plastic spoon under his belt. When Ronnie asked why, he said, 'You never know when it will come in useful; it can be used as a spade or a weapon or lots of things.' They jumped out onto the pavement and set off to find the zoo. Ronnie flew alongside Thomas but was always on his guard just in case a bird tried to eat him, and they ran from one hiding place to another.

Eventually, Thomas said, 'I think we are near, I can hear animal noises and smell animal smells. I think if we go round the next corner we will be there.'

They were right. There were lots of people waiting in a queue to get inside and there was about twenty mummies and daddies tickling their children, who were laughing, and some were saying, 'Please stop or I might wet myself,' but they just carried on.

Thomas said, 'The ticklefish are here. They will soon be everywhere, having fun tickling children. I think we should sneak into the zoo quickly while people are tickling their children.' So they ran as fast as they could into the zoo without any trouble. They started going round the zoo looking at all the different animals, but if people saw Thomas they either thought he was a mouse and were frightened and ran away, or they tried to bash him, or they thought he was an escaped animal and tried to catch him.

Ronnie was fed up of people trying to swat him and said to Thomas, 'Let's find somewhere to hide quickly, I'm fed up of this.' So they climbed into the first cage they could and hid in the straw in the cage.

'I don't like it in London,' Ronnie said. 'I am thinking of going back to sea. If I find a ship like Captain Welk has, I will sneak on board and it should be safer for me. Are you coming with me?'

'I don't think so,' said Thomas. 'I didn't like it at sea, but it will be so sad to see you go. Will you stay with me just long enough to find my way?'

'Of course,' said Ronnie, 'we will always be friends and if ever you need me when I have gone, I am going to give you three wishes, but you must use them wisely.'

'Oh, thank you very much,' Thomas said. 'I will look after them very very carefully, and I would like you to have some of my troll toffee. It will make you strong and brave if you need it.'

Then they settled down under the straw and had a nice sleep. Thomas was woken up suddenly by someone breathing hot air on him; when he opened his eyes, he saw a lion looking down at him, licking his lips. He very carefully nudged Ronnie, who looked up and saw the lion and said, 'What are we going to do now?'

'I don't know,' Thomas said.

'I do,' said Ronnie. 'I will distract him and you run.' Then he flew up and landed on the lion's nose and started pulling his whiskers, which made the lion sneeze. As a matter of fact, he sneezed that hard that he blew Thomas out of the cage. Ronnie flew after Thomas and they both left the zoo quickly.

'I am definitely going back to sea,' Ronnie said.

'And I am definitely leaving London,' said Thomas, 'but which way do I go?'

They both set off walking and looking for something to eat and rest when Ronnie pointed to a big garden. 'Let's have a look in there,' he said, and they both went into the garden and looked around. Then Thomas just stopped and stared.

'What are you looking at?' asked Ronnie.

'Look over there by that tree, another troll! I am going to say hello, are you coming?' Thomas asked.

'Yes,' said Ronnie, but as they got closer they saw that it was made of stone.

They went up close to it and Thomas said, 'Look, it's a girl troll, she must have got caught in the sun. Just look at her, she is the most beautiful girl I have seen. Look at her lovely big crooked nose with four warts, and look at those beautiful big ears with the hair coming out, and there's her lovely bushy eyebrows and her scraggly hair, and what is most beautiful of all is her enormous front teeth. Oh, how I wish she wasn't stone,' Thomas said. 'Could I use one of those wishes you gave me to make her real, or am I not being careful enough?'

'Well, I think if we made her real again she could be your friend when I go and live on Captain Willy Welks' ship. I know, I will cast a spell that will make her real and able to go in the sun just like you. But it is a very hard spell and will take up nearly all my energy, so we will have to rest for the night in this garden.'

'All right,' said Thomas, 'I will stand guard all night for you.'

So Ronnie went up to the girl troll and said, 'Oh elf God, sat on your mighty throne, make this troll real and not of stone.'

Ronnie lifted his hands to the sky and lightning flew from his fingertips up to the clouds, and the elf God said, 'Why do you want this, Ronnie? She is a troll not an elf.'

Ronnie answered, 'Yes, elf God, but my best friend Thomas is a troll and he has helped me lots of times and we are about to go our separate ways. She will be company for him.'

'Well, if he has been that good to you I will grant you that wish.'

Ronnie sat on the floor, tired out with all the magic it had taken, then there was a loud noise like a jet engine then everything went very quiet. Thomas looked over at the girl troll, but she was just the same; then, slowly, he saw her changing colour. Her skin was becoming the colour of a troll. Then she blinked and moved her head. Thomas was so excited he didn't know what to do, he just stood staring at her thinking she was the most beautiful troll in the world.

Thomas looked at Ronnie and saw that he was tired out after all his hard work. So he started helping him to his feet, but he was very wobbly. Out of the corner of his eye, he saw the girl troll slowly coming toward them, and Thomas said to her, 'Will you help us please? We have to find somewhere safe for my friend to rest.'

The girl troll went over to them and helped Ronnie to his feet and said, 'I know just the place, but when we are there, will you please tell me why you did this for me?'

'How do you know what we did?' asked Thomas.

'I know I had turned to stone, but you can still see things and hear things, and what you and your friend did for me is very brave.'

They both helped Ronnie to the base of a huge oak tree, which had a little hole in the trunk which they went through, and inside there was a bed and wood for a fire and everything a troll could need. 'This is where I used to live until I turned to stone.' She went over to the bed and checked that the straw in the mattress hadn't got damp and there was nothing that would hurt Ronnie, then she helped him on the bed, tucked him up with an old dish cloth, and said, 'Thank you for saving me, now go to sleep, you are safe.'

While Ronnie was sleeping, Thomas said, 'My name is Thomas and he is my best friend, Ronnie. Can I ask your name please?'

'My name is Tracy,' she said. 'Why did you save me?'

Thomas turned red and went shy and didn't know what to say; after all, he had never had a girlfriend, he was only sixty.

He started stuttering his words and sweating. Tracy said, 'Are you all right, Thomas?' and touched his cheek, and Thomas thought he was going to faint his heart was beating so fast.

'I don't know what's wrong,' he said, 'maybe I have caught a human cold.'

'Well, if so, we will have to cuddle up close to keep you warm.'

'No,' he said, 'I might pass it to you.'

'Shall we just talk about why you saved me?' Tracy asked. 'It might take your mind off your cold.'

Thomas realised it wasn't a cold. He wanted to be Tracy's boyfriend, but he didn't know what to say. *What shall I say now?* he thought. *I'm only sixty, isn't that too young to have a girlfriend? But if I don't do anything, she might meet another troll, or even worse, she might go back to Norway and meet someone there.* Thomas took a deep breath and told her about his and Ronnie's adventures and how Ronnie didn't like England and was going back to sea. Then he told Tracy that he saw her and thought she was the most beautiful girl troll he had seen.

Tracy started to giggle shyly and blush, and she whispered, 'Thank you.'

This surprised Thomas and made him feel good, so he said, 'Ronnie thought we could be friends and go on adventures together when he leaves.' Then Thomas said, 'Now I have met you, I hope that one day you will be my girlfriend.'

Tracy said, 'I would love to go on adventures with you and will be your girlfriend anytime.'

***

In the morning when they had all had a sleep and Ronnie was wide awake, Thomas told Ronnie that he and Tracy were going on their adventures as soon as Ronnie felt strong enough to go back to sea. Ronnie said that he was ready now and that he had good fun with Thomas but was fed up of people trying to swat him, but he was sure they would meet again one day.

Tracy and Thomas both gave Ronnie a big kiss and cuddle, then waved as he flew off. Then they looked at each other, and Tracy said, 'What shall we do now?'

Thomas said, 'Shall we start our new adventures?'

Tracy said, 'Yes please,' and gave Thomas a kiss on the cheek and said, 'Thank you for saving me.' Then Thomas and Tracy set off holding hands, wondering what their next adventure would be.

PART TWO

Both Thomas and Tracy walked in the sun without turning to stone and they were telling each other about the things they had done. Thomas told Tracy about the time he was at the Great Elder's hundred and nineteenth birthday parade and all the town were lining the streets to cheer and sing happy birthday to the Great Elder, and Thomas had put a whoopee cushion under the cushion on his throne and when he sat down it sounded as if he had pumped. 'The Great Elder was angry, but he never knew it was me,' Thomas said. 'And then there was the time I had a ticklefish as a pet and trained it to tickle Tarquin Troll's guard dogs and all they could do was ROAR with laughter. Tarquin is a very posh troll and it's good fun teasing him. Did you have any fun in Troll Town while you were there, Tracy?' asked Thomas.

'I had some fun, but I enjoyed school and learning things. I can do adding and subtraction and my times table. I can read and write, I can even read in English.'

'Wow,' said Thomas, 'you must be very clever, I wish I could read English. When we stop for the night will you teach me please?'

'It will take more than one night, but we can make a start,' Tracy said.

They walked and talked and before they knew it, the sun was setting and they started to look for somewhere safe warm and dry to stop for the night. They found a nice big garden with plenty of nettles to eat. Trolls love nettles; they don't sting them and they taste like sweets. Thomas started to run towards them and Tracy said to him sternly, 'Thomas, you are not allowed nettles until you have had some dandelions first. As long as you are my boyfriend you will eat properly.'

Thomas went back to Tracy and said, 'Am I really your boyfriend?'

When Tracy said yes, his little heart fluttered and he felt ever so proud; he was even brave enough to hold Tracy's hand. They walked around the garden and found a nice safe corner of garden to stay the night. Tracy said, 'You go and get some dandelions and some nettles for our tea, and I will make a comfy straw mattress for us to sleep on.' Just before Thomas started his chores, Tracy said, 'Don't forget, no extra nettles until you've had your main meal.'

Thomas skipped off to get their food thinking how lovely Tracy was, and he got everything as quick as he could. He even managed to get a pot of water from the pond, then rushed back to Tracy with a big smile on his face. Tracy had been busy too; she had made a lovely thick bed for them out of straw and grass and she had found a piece of tea towel to use as a blanket, which looked ever so comfy.

They both sat down and had a lovely tea together. Thomas didn't want it to end and ate far too much. When he couldn't eat any more, he let out a noisy burp and blushed. Tracy tried to tell him off but giggled instead.

After tea, Tracy said to Thomas, 'Are you ready to start to learn to read? I really think you should. If we have half an hour a day after tea, that would leave us time to explore and make plans before bedtime.'

So they both sat down and Tracy started to teach Thomas the alphabet, which he found hard to learn because he would rather be playing. After the lesson, he had learnt ABCD, and Tracy told him he would have to try a bit harder next time. Thomas agreed, but said that he didn't like school.

They both explored the garden and found a stone gnome. Thomas asked Tracy if she thought it was a real one that had got caught in the sun.

'I don't know if gnomes turn to stone like us.'

'Shall we see if we can find out?'

'Yes but not tonight,' Tracy said, 'it's been a lovely day but I am tired now. I would like to snuggle up in bed and go to sleep.'

So they both laid on the mattress and Thomas said, 'This is lovely and comfy and warm. I think we will be safe here anyway. I will look after you, Tracy. Night night.'

When he looked at Tracy, he saw that she was already asleep and snoring, which to a troll was a lovely gargling noise and it soon sent Thomas to sleep.

Thomas was woken during the night and peeped out over the blanket and saw a cat looking round. He immediately grabbed a piece of troll toffee in case he needed it. But he didn't, because he heard somebody shout and the cat ran off. Thomas looked into the dark and thought he saw the gnome walking round, but wasn't sure if he was dreaming.He thought, *I will speak to Tracy in the morning*, and went back to sleep.

When they woke up in the morningthere was a plate with four big juicy sausages and two pieces of bread. Thomas and Tracy looked at each other and both said at the same time, 'Where did you get that from?'

Then they both said, 'I didn't get it, but it looks lovely, shall we eat it?'

'I can't see anybody else around and I am starving,' Tracy said, so they stayed on the bed and ate every little bit. After breakfast, Thomas told Tracy about what had happened during the night Tracy thought a moment and then said, 'Do you think we have eaten the gnome's breakfast?'

'I hope not, we don't even know if he is real yet,' Thomas said, 'but we could stay for another night and try to find out.'So they decided to stay another night where they were and explore the other gardens that were around.

Thomas wanted to go straight away but Tracy said to him, 'Listen, Thomas, I know you're only sixty but you are going to have to learn a few things while we are in England. A lot of humans love their gardens and keep them clean and tidy, so if we just leave here now you can bet that when we come back our bed will have been thrown away and the human will be watching to see what had made it, so if we tidy it away now we should be able to come back later and make it again.'

Thomas thought to himself, *I hope I am as clever as Tracy when I grow up. I shall have to listen to her carefully instead of thinking about exploring all the time.* So they tidied everything away and then Thomas asked what they should do next.

Tracy said, 'Well, I think we should have a look round the garden next door to start.'

As they were going to the garden next door they walked past the gnome. They stopped and Thomas said, 'If you left that breakfast for us, thank you very much, it was really nice. And I don't know if it was you that chased that cat away but if it was, thanks again, it was really brave of you. And one more thing: we are staying in the garden tonight so you are welcome to come and see us.'

As they turned, Thomas looked at him and saw him wink. When they were in the garden next door Thomas told Tracy about the gnome winking at him and she chuckled and gave Thomas a cuddle. She said, 'You are lovely, don't ever change, will you? Your imagination is the best there is.'

Thomas said to her, 'Just wait and see, he will visit us tonight.'

They found the garden they were in boring, and they were just lazing around under a bush when Tracy said, 'Look, there are names on the ends of streets. I know a game we can play, we can sneak along the streets so nobody sees us and I will teach you to read the street name.'

Thomas got very excited and said, 'That is a brilliant game, come on quick, let's go.'

'Well, let's start with this street. Look over the road, there is the name fastened to the wall. You learnt the first two letters last night, remember?'

Thomas thought hard. 'Then is the first one B and the second A?'

'Yes,' said Tracy, 'Now the third one is K, and I think the best way to remember that is kicking K because it has two legs sticking out. Now, if you can learn one more letter I will tell you the rest.'

'All right,' said Thomas, 'but can I learn more like this, it's good fun.'

'OK,' said Tracy, 'if you can remember this letter we will carry on. The next letter is E. Look how it's got three little legs. If you can remember like that, it can help. Do you want to try the last two letters and then you will have learnt your first word in English?'

Thomas said, 'Yes please, but can we learn more this way later please?'

'All right, if you can read the word after the last two letters we will carry on this way . Now the next is R, it looks a bit like head with two legs. And the last letter is Y and that looks a bit like a windmill. So do you think you can read that, Thomas?'

Thomas looked long and hard at the sign and started to laugh.

'What are you laughing at?' Tracy asked sternly. 'It's not a funny name.'

'No, but it will be a funny street. I have just seen a shoal of ticklefish going to that house so before long there will be ticklefish everywhere.'

'Well, now just concentrate on that word and that will be your lesson over for now.'

Thomas said, 'B. A. K. E. R. Y. Ba... bake... bakery? Is it bakery? Am I right?' Thomas asked excitedly. 'Please say I am right.'

Tracy said, 'You have just learnt your firstword in English, shall I tell you the second?'

Thomas was jumping for joy and said, 'Yes please.'

'Well, the second word is lane. So this street is called Bakery Lane. And all the houses will be full of ticklefish.'

'Oh, thank you for teaching me my first word,' and he ran over and gave Tracy a kiss and cuddle. When he realised what he had done he went bright red.

Tracy said to him, 'You mustn't get embarrassed by showing affection, everything does it in their own way. Cats, rabbits, even troll terriers; everything. And don't forget I am your girlfriend.'

'I know,' said Thomas, 'but you're the first girlfriend I have ever had and I didn't know if I was doing the right thing.' Thomas was shaking with excitement, his heart was beating about two hundred times a minute, and he said, 'I must be the happiest troll alive.'

They both decided to go back to their own garden and rest, because they were going to stay up all night to see if the gnome was real and would he come and visit. They found a shaded place under a rose bush with big red roses on and nice big thorns that would make it hard for anything to creep up on them. It was a lovely warm day, and they both just lay on their tummies watching all the garden animals.

The next thing they knew, it was dark and the gnome was sat under the rose bush with them. Tracy saw him first and she was frightened; he was a lot bigger than her and had a long white beard, a red pointed hat, a green coat with a belt, and red trousers. She grabbed hold of Thomas and shook his arm, saying, 'Wake up, Thomas, we have a visitor and I am scared.'

When Thomas had woken up and saw the gnome, he said to Tracy, 'Don't be silly, he won't hurt us, look at his friendly smile.'

The gnome said in a deep and gentle voice, 'Hello little trolls, I am pleased to meet you, my name is Wilhelm. Can I ask what your names are?'

Thomas told Wilhelm their names and asked him if he had left the breakfast and made the cat go away. Wilhelm nodded and said it was. Thomas thanked him very much. 'But why did you do that?' he asked, 'and I hope you don't mind me saying, you have got an unusual name. Will you tell us all about yourself please?'

'What would you like to know?' said Wilhelm.

'Well, what are you doing here? Where do you come from? Things like that.'

'Well the gnome people originally come from a place called Germany. We used to live on farms and help the farmers look after their crops.'

'How did you help?' said Tracy.

'All gnomes are mystical and can do wizardry, but they only do that if they have to. They normally just use magic to help other creatures.'

'So is it mysticism that makes you look and feel like stone?' Tracy asked. 'What are you doing in England?'

Wilhelm told them about how he and thousands of other gnomes came to England because the gnome tribe was getting too big and there wasn't enough work for everyone.

'So that's why you fed us and made that cat go away, are all gnomes friendly and kind like you?'

'We all try to be friendly but there are quite a few of us that can be naughty and play tricks on humans. Tricks like, we will sometimes move to a new place in the garden, then they search all over for us and when they are not looking we move back where we were. It's hard not to laugh when you see them scratching their heads and wondering what has just happened.'

Thomas thought that was great fun and said, 'I will have to remember that.'

'But gnomes always help others if they can, that way if we need help somebody might help us. Anyway,' said Wilhelm, 'I will have to go to work. The cat from next door comes every night making a mess and scaring little creatures, so I will see you later and don't forget, if you see me I might look like stone and might not move, but I am real.'

When Wilhelm had gone to work, Tracy said, 'Right, Thomas, it's time for your reading lesson, let's go and find a sign to learn.'

They left the garden and because it was dark, they didn't have to hide. As they were looking round, Thomas said, 'Where do you think we should go next?'

Tracy said, 'I don't know,' then her eyes widened and a big grin appeared on her face and she said, 'I do know. Do you see that sign fastened on that post? I will teach you to read it, and that's the way we go.'

Now Thomas was really in a muddle. He said he had no idea what she was talking about.

'Just wait till I have taught you to read it, then you will understand.'

So the two of them sat under a tree and Thomas listened very carefully to Tracy and in no time he had learnt two words: the words north and west.

'I know about getting to places using north, south, east and west, but why do humans put signs up like that?'

'It's to help them find their way when they're driving their cars, and it also means that we can follow that sign as well.'

'Right, then we will go back to the garden, have a long rest, and then when it is dark again we will set off. I do love adventures,' Thomas said. 'Do you think we should ask Wilhelm if he wants to come with us?'

'Yes, let's,' Tracy said, 'he might like a change of scenery.'

So they went back to the garden and looked around for Wilhelm.They found him stood next to the pond holding a fishing rod. He wasn't moving at all so Thomas went up to him and whispered, 'When you have finished work will you come and see us please?'

Wilhelm didn't say anything, just winked again, so they left him and went back to their little corner of the garden and made their comfy bed and waited for Wilhelm.

When Wilhelm arrived after work he said in his deep quiet voice, 'Hi, my little troll friends, what do you want to see me about?'

Thomas told him they were moving on and asked if he would like to come with them. Thomas also asked why he was fishing at night. Wilhelm replied, 'Well, first of all, Thomas, I wasn't really fishing, I haven't got any hooks on my rod. I was just waiting for the cat to come and try to catch a fish. When it comes, I make a noise like a big dog growling that frightens her off. I don't mind anything hunting for their food but when they get their food from humans they don't need any more. And as for moving on, I can understand why you want to go, you are young, full of mischief, and you want to explore . But are you ready? Have you got everything you need?'

Thomas said, 'We can go out in the daylight without turning to stone, and I have three wishes given to me by Ronnie the elf. I also have my troll toffee.'

'And we will look after each other,' Tracy said.

'Well, it sounds to me you are ready to go and I hope you have a really happy time together. But I will not be travelling with you, I have done all the travelling I want. I am too old now, and this garden is my kingdom. I look after it and the other animals that live in it,' Wilhelm said. 'But thank you for asking me. And I have a gift for you both that might be very useful on your travels.'

Tracy said, 'Thank you very much, but can I ask what it is?'

'Well,' Wilhelm said, 'it's a very special gnome gift. It is a saying that you repeat to any gnome anywhere in the world. But before I tell you it, you must promise with all of your heart that you will not tell anybody about it and only share it with other gnomes.'

Tracy and Thomas both promised not to tell anybody but other gnomes, and only if they were in trouble. 'Right,' said Wilhelm, 'Are you ready... ah, no, I will write it down, you never know who is listening.' So he wrote it down and Tracy and Thomas said they would both learn it before they set off and give him the code back.

Thomas couldn't read it all, so Tracy had to whisper it very quietly in his ear until he had learnt it. The only trouble was, every time she tried to whisper her long crooked nose got tickled by the hair sticking out of his ear, which made her sneeze and giggle so it took a long time for Thomas to learn it. Tracy asked Thomas if he had learnt the saying off by heart, and he said he had. She said to him, 'Well, tell me it just to make sure.'

So Thomas said, 'Oh, lovely...'

Tracy said quickly, 'Shhh, Thomas, you're saying it too loud, whisper it.'

So Thomas said it quietly in Tracy's ear and he had got it right. They both sat down and talked about where they would go next, and decided that they would travel at nighttime because it would be safer. They collected all belongings and tidied up their little den they had made, then went to find Wilhelm.

He was talking to two little field mice; he was telling them that they could stay in the garden and have some supper, but they were not to eat the best plants because the humans would be upset and might put traps out to try and catch them. The little mice said thank you and scampered off into the garden, Tracy told Wilhelm about their plans and said they were going to rest somewhere all day and go at nighttime.

Wilhelm said to them that they should rest in the hedge that goes round the front of the garden, and that he would keep them safe until it was time to go. So they all said goodbye to each other and had a cuddle, then Thomas and Tracy found a nice comfy place under the hedge and went to sleep.

***

When they woke up, they were both excited and wanted to start their new adventure so they got everything they needed and found Wilhelm, who was now sat on a doorstep with a big smile on his face, with a bottle of milk with the cream missing. 'The humans will blame the birds,' he said.

Tracy told him they were about to set off so they all had another cuddle then Tracy and Thomas set off on a new adventure.

PART THREE

As they walked along the road towards north west, they chatted happily and held hands. They were saying it would be great fun to see new parts of England. When Thomas saw a sign with an arrow pointing on it, he asked Tracy what it said. She looked at the sign and told Thomas it said Buckingham Palace, and the arrow was pointing the way to go. 'That is a very important place, it's where the Queen of England lives.'

Thomas said, 'Come on, let's go and have look at it, we might see the Queen.' So off they went, following the signs to Buckingham Palace. Eventually they got there just in time to see a guardsmen stood in his sentry box, trying not to laugh. Both Thomas and Tracy saw three ticklefish under his nose and at least six in his furry hat. Then they saw the big palace with all the lights on and a really posh flag.

'What is that flag?' asked Thomas. 'That is the royal standard and it only flies when the Queen is staying there, I think we should sneak in and hide because it's nearly daytime and we might see the Queen,' Tracy said.

'But what happens if we get caught? Will we be put in jail? Come on,' Thomas said. 'Tracy, look, there are railings over there we can climb up that little bit of wall and jump through the railings.'

They both checked that the way was clear, then ran as fast as they could, climbed the little wall, and jumped through the railings. Then they heard the guardsmen start to laugh. He was laughing so much that his sergeant marched up and shouted at him but the ticklefish started tickling the sergeant and he starting laughing as well and anybody that came to see what was going on was tickled, and soon there was a crowd of humans all laughing so much; some of them were crying, some were holding their tummies, there were even some rolling on the floor. While all this was going on Tracy and Thomas sneaked off to a huge garden, but they were laughing so much they couldn't see properly and fell into a water fountain, which made them laugh even more.

When they had stopped laughing, they climbed out of the fountain and Thomas said, 'Well, that's my monthly bath. Let's hope it's going to be a warm day, then we will dry off quickly. Shall we go and find a good hiding place to watch for the Queen?'

'Yes,' said Tracy, 'and I hope my hair doesn't get all frizzy from getting wet.'

They found a beautiful flower garden as near to the palace as they dare go and they had to check very carefully that nobody was around before they sneaked into it. They lay down on their tummies; that is the best way for trolls, because if they get tired they can rest their head on their long crooked nose and have a rest.

Tracy heard talking and looked and saw two humans coming toward them. She said, 'Thomas, quickly, what shall we do?'

Thomas looked and said, 'They look like gardeners and they are coming to this garden. There is only one thing to do, and that's use one of the spells.'

'Oh, hurry up, Thomas, I think they have seen us.'

'You are right, they have. Stand still, I am about to cast a spell.'

Both of them stood up and said, 'Oh elf God, come down from your throne and grant us my wish that we look like stone.'

There was a rumble of thunder and a flash of lightning. Thomas and Tracy felt their skin change colour and it felt like stone. Then they heard a gardener say, 'I wonder who put those trolls there. I think we should move them somewhere else because I think it is going to rain with all that thunder and lightning.'

'Where shall we put them?' asked the other gardener.

'I know, let's put on the step by the front door of the palace. I think the Queen likes trolls.'

So they picked up Tracy and Thomas and placed them side by side on the top step right outside the palace entrance. Tracy asked, 'What do we do now, Thomas?' And he replied, 'I think we should just stay here for a while, we are in the perfect place to see the Queen if she comes out, and we can help guard the palace. I will pass you a piece of toffee if you would like.'

Tracy said, 'Yes please, but I don't think I will need it when you are with me, I think you are brave enough for both of us. But don't forget to make sure nobody is watching before you move.'

They both had a sneaky look round and nobody was watching them so he passed Tracy a piece of toffee and quickly put in her bag. Then she said, 'Isn't this so exciting, watching all the soldiers and other humans at work or talking or just sitting in the sun? Look, they are having a picnic outside the walls of the palace. I wonder why.'

'Perhaps they are hoping to see the Queen as well but haven't managed to sneak in like we did, but you are right, it is very exciting,' Thomas said. So they just stayed on the step watching everything they could. But they were that busy watching some humans trying to shoo away some ticklefish, they never heard the door open to the palace and a lady with four dogs came out. The dogs went straight over to Tracy and Thomas and sniffed them then they licked them.

Then the lady said, 'Ohh, trolls, how lovely, where did they come from?' to a man that was with her.

'I don't know, ma'am,' he said.

Then the lady said, 'Well they do look nice there,' and said to her doggies, 'come along, let's go walkies.'

When they had gone, both Thomas and Tracy were shaking with excitement. Tracy said, 'I think that was the Queen.'

'So do I,' Thomas said, 'and she likes us being here. I think we should stay here forever.'

'Well,' Tracy said, 'we will talk about that later, but we should be careful for now and not move around.I've noticed one of the guardsmen keeps looking at us.'

So they both stood very still until night time, and then

Thomas said, 'I think we should go back to the garden and get some flowers, I am starving.'

They both looked around and couldn't see anybody, so they sneaked down the steps and ran as fast as they could towards the garden. They ran round a corner and just as they got round, the guardsmen that had been watching them threw a net over them. The more they struggled the more they got tangled up in the net, so they just lay there as the guardsmen looked at them and finally he said, 'So you are real. And I thought trolls were just statues. Now I have caught you, I will have to think what I can do with you.'

'You can't do anything with us, the lady that came out of the palace said she liked us and she will not allow it,' Thomas shouted.

'I will have to go and see my sergeant about this,' the guardsmen answered, 'but until then I will put you in jail in the Tower of London.'

The guardsmen picked them both up by their tails and carried them to the palace gates where a policeman was stood. The guardsmen said to him, 'I just caught two trolls and they are real, not statues. Can you take them to the Tower of London for me and ask the soldiers there to put them jail until I have spoken to my sergeant?'

The policeman said, 'You are kidding me, there is no such thing as real trolls.'

'What are these then?' and he held Thomas and Tracy by their tails. When he did, the policeman said, 'Blimey, they're ugly, aren't they.'

Both Thomas and Tracy were very upset at being called ugly and they both hissed at the policeman like a snake. The policeman just laughed at them and said to the guardsmen, 'Will I be safe with such angry prisoners?' Then he took them both over to his police van, threw them in the back, and said to the guardsmen, 'Tell the soldiers at the Tower of London I am on my way.'

On their way there, Thomas said, 'Don't worry Tracy, everything will be all right, the Queen will tell them to let us go, and if she doesn't we will escape. Don't forget we have troll toffee, two wishes, and our secret code for the gnomes. Can you remember it?' he asked Tracy.

'Yes, of course I can. Can you?'

'Of course I can,' Thomas said. 'It's "Oh lovely gnome Oh friendly gnome"...'

'SHHHH!' Tracy said. 'That policeman might hear you, you really will have to remember to be careful what you say.'

'Oops, I am sorry,' Thomas said, 'but you are right, I will have to be careful.'

When they got to the jail, the policeman said to the guardsmen on duty, 'Where do you want these two naughty trolls?'

The guardsmen said, 'Are they real, or has someone dressed up their pet guinea pigs?'

'They are real,' said the policeman, 'and they were caught trying to get into Buckingham Palace.'

'Well in that case, we had better put them in the same jail that Anne Boleyn was in.'

***

When they were in jail Thomas looked around and in one corner there was a pile of straw and an old blanket. Thomas said to the guardsmen, 'Do you feed us in here?'

They were told they got bread and water three times a day, and at night they should save some in case the ghost of Anne Boleyn came to visit them. Tracy ran over to the blanket and hid under it and the guardsmen laughed and said, 'Don't worry, she will only eat you if there is no bread left.'

Thomas went over to Tracy and said, 'There is nothing to be scared of, I don't even know who Anne Boleyn was so she can't be that scary can she?'

Tracy popped her head out from under the blanket and said, 'She was married to the king of England hundreds of years ago, and he wanted to marry somebody else so he said she was very very naughty and had her head chopped off.'

'Well,' said Thomas, 'it sounds to me that the king was the naughty one, not her, and if she does visit,she can have some of our bread and water with pleasure. But it is nearly daytime, and we might have been let out by tonight.'

'Oh, I do hope so, I have never met a ghost before, especially one that was married to a King. She might be ever so posh and I will not know what to do.'

'Listen,' said Thomas, 'we might not be here, if we are, Anne Boleyn might not come to visit, and if she does, I don't think we have got anything to be frightened of, so please don't worry. I will look after you.'

At eight o'clock the guardsmen brought them their bread and water for breakfast and he teased them that if they didn't save any for the ghost, she might eat them. Tracy was scared, but Thomas said, 'Look, my friend is shaking with cold, can we borrow your furry hat to keep her warm? And where is the pom pom off it?'

The guardsman's face went bright red with anger and he shouted and pointed to his hat, saying, 'This is not a pom pom hat, this is a royal guardsman's hat, it makes us very important soldiers.'

Thomas answered him, 'Well, you had better be careful then, because if a guardsman's kept her prisoner she might eat you.'

The guardsman looked at Thomas and then turned away and didnt talk to him anymore because he was scared in case Thomas was right.

Thomas said to Tracy, 'I don't think he will try to scare us again. Let's have breakfast and then we can save our energy for when we get out of this jail.' When it was dinner time and the guardsman came with it, he never said anything about ghosts. Thomas asked, 'Have you spoken to the Queen about us yet?'

'The Queen is a very busy lady, you might be in here for weeks before she gets time to see you.'

When he had gone, Tracy said to Thomas, 'We will not be in here weeks, will we, you will get us out soon, won't you?'

Thomas answered, 'I have a plan in my head that we can use tonight if we are still here, but once we have got out we will follow the north star because there might be a reward for anybody that catches us and we will have to get away from London.'

'Oh, I don't know what I would do without you, Thomas. What is your plan?'

'Well, can you see our prison door? It's made of old wood with a hole in the top with iron bars in. Well, tonight we will have a little toffee climb up the old door go through the bars and hide in the guardsman's hat.'

'But why follow the north star?' Tracy asked.

'Because,' Thomas said, 'We will be nearer our own country, Norway, and hopefully whatever the place is called it will be friendlier.'

'The place where you are talking about is called Scotland, I have never been but I have read about it and from what I understand the men must be very tough because they wear a thing called a kilt. It's a bit like a skirt but they don't wear anything under it and if the winter is like it is in Norway, they will get a very cold bottom.'

They were just relaxing on the bed of straw when the guardsman came with their tea and Thomas said to him, 'I hope you have put enough on for the ghost of Anne Boleyn, because if she is hungry she might eat you.'

The guardsman said, 'If you don't tell anybody that I am scared of ghosts, I will get you some more.' He went down to the kitchen and came back with three pieces of chocolate cake and said, 'There's a piece for each of you and one for the ghost.'

'Thank you very much, it looks lovely,' Tracy told the guardsman.

He said, 'Please don't tell anyone, because the other soldiers will tease me if they know I am scared of ghosts.' Both Thomas and Tracy both smiled mischievously at the guardsman and nodded. They sat down and ate their tea but saved some for the ghost if she came. Tracy was very nervous because she didn't know what would happen, but Thomas said there was nothing to worry about; he would look after her, and hold her hand. Tracy snuggled up close to Thomas and she didn't feel as scared knowing he was there. They just sat in the dark waiting, then in one corner of the jail a lady appeared out of nowhere.

Thomas just stared at her; he couldn't believe what he had just seen. Tracy buried her head against Thomas, as she didn't want to look. The lady said to them, 'Hello, I am Anne Boleyn. I was once married to Henry the Eighth, the King of England, but he went off me and made up stories about me. Then made a man come from France and chop my head off.'

Thomas said to her, 'But your head is on your shoulders, Your Highness.'

She replied, 'Please call me Anne, I do not want to be Highness anymore, and after so many years I can balance my head on my shoulders. I just have to be careful how I sit and bend over. What is wrong with your friend?' she asked Thomas.

'Can I introduce myself and my friend and will you sit with us please and have some supper?'

'I would love to, thank you,' Anne said.

After Anne sat down Thomas told her all about their travels and how they ended up in jail, and that Tracy was scared in case ghosts were horrible. Anne said to Tracy, 'You must not be afraid of ghosts, they are people that have gone to heaven and they only appear when nice people are around like yourself.'

Tracy looked at Anne shyly and whispered, 'But what about the bad ghosts?'

Anne replied, 'I have never met a bad ghost, only mischievous ones. The bad ones are not allowed in heaven and that is where ghosts live.'

'So ghosts won't hurt anybody then?' Tracy said.

'No, they might make you jump or frighten you but that is just the way they play. I will show you later. Do you want to escape from here?' Anne said to both of them.

Tracy answered, 'Yes, Thomas has made a plan for tonight.'

'Well, I will get you out by being mischievous. You watch what I do after our tea has settled.'

They all had a little nap and after an hour or so, Anne said, 'Are you ready to escape, then?' They both started to get fidgety and said yes. 'Right, well, just you watch this,' said Anne, and picked them up and put them on a ledge in the wall so they could see out of the hole in the door. Then Anne gave them a lovely friendly smile and floated through the door. She came out of the other side and tapped the guardsman on the shoulder and said to him, 'I am the ghost of Anne Boleyn. Will you look after my head while I break down this door to let my friends out?'

The guardsmen jumped with fright and said, 'Please don't take your head off, I am already the most scared person in the Tower and I will do anything you ask but please don't frighten me anymore.'

'Alright,' said Anne. 'I want you to unlock the jail and let my friends out. Then I want you to stay inside, lock the door, and put the key through the hole with bars in.'

'But then I will be stuck in the jail,' answered the guardsmen.

'And that is just what I want. Then in the morning you can tell your sergeant that my friends escaped and locked you in, or I will let them know you are a sissy soldier and frightened of ghosts,' said Anne.

The guardsmen did just what Anne said, and she laughed and said to Thomas and Tracy, 'Ohh, I did enjoy that, it was good ghost fun and I didn't hurt anybody did I?'

Tracy had a big grin on her face and said, 'No, and I will never be afraid of ghosts again.'

Anne said to them both, 'I am going to put you outside the walls of the Tower of London and point you in the direction you should go. It has been lovely meeting you and I haven't had so much fun for about a hundred years.

The next thing both Thomas and Tracy knew is that they were stood on a street in London, and Anne pointed north and said, 'Goodbye, my little friends,' and disappeared.

They both set off walking as fast as they could. Thomas was excited. Tracy was scared again. Thomas told Tracy not to be silly, he would look after her, so they just carried on walking until the morning and they were tired out and their feet and legs hurt. They picked some beautiful young buttercups and Thomas's favourites, some nice nettles. Tracy found a plastic bottle that had some rain water in so they found a nice little hiding place and had their breakfast and a good long sleep.

When they woke up they drank the last of the water and waited for it to get dark. Tracy said, 'Will we have to walk a long way tonight? My feet and legs still ache.'

'Well, we can still see London and I will not feel safe until we are a long way from it. And when we get to the countryside we can walk in the daytime when the sun is shining and nobody will see us if we stay in long grass like this.'

'All right,' said Tracy, 'if we must go tonight we had better go now.'

They both set off, walking slowly. Thomas tried to make Tracy happy but she was a real grumpy pants, so he kept quiet and walked behind her so he could make sure she was all right. After they had walked for a long time, Tracy sat down and said, 'That is it, I can't take another step.' They both sat down in the grass near the edge of the road. Tracy put her head on Thomas's legs and fell straight to sleep. He listened to her snore and thought, *what a lovely sound, I hope she never leaves me.* As he sat looking round at all the traffic, he watched lorries going into a car park and the drivers get out and go into a building. He thought to himself, *I think we should go and see what is happening after Tracy has had a little rest.*

When Tracy woke up it was nearly daylight, so they went to where the lorries were as quick as they could. Thomas saw a lorry with curtains on the side which were tied down with string. He said to Tracy, 'Do you think you can climb onto that lorry?'

She answered him, 'If you help me and it means we can have a rest, I can.'

Both of them climbed up onto the back of the lorry and when Thomas saw what was in it, his eyes nearly popped out: it was full to the top with everything a troll could want. There were sweets, biscuits, chocolate ice cream in a big freezer, all kinds of pop, everything you need. The first thing they did was find some marshmallows and make a comfy place to sit, then Thomas started looking for some chocolate and some pop, but Tracy said to him, 'You can leave those alone, you have only just had your breakfast. You are a troll, not a pig, and as long as you are my troll boyfriend you do as I say!'

Thomas was really fed up and stamped his feet in a tantrum, and Tracy said, 'I am only doing this because I care for you and want you to stay healthy.' But Thomas bowed his head to the floor, went to the corner of the lorry and sat down with a bump. 'Please yourself,' Tracy said, 'and when you are feeling happier I will be on this nice comfy marshmallow seat having a sleep. There is room for both of us to snuggle up and keep warm and comfy.'

Thomas stayed in the corner until the lorry set off and then he started to get happier about the next part of the journey, and he thought maybe they could have chocolate and pop for dinner. He went over Tracy and said he was sorry for having a tantrum, and could he snuggle up next to her on the marshmallow seat? She said of course he could he could snuggle up to her anytime he wanted, but he had to understand she was trying to look after him. Both of them were really happy together in the lorry with all the nice smells and the bumping of the lorry as it went along the road. They just lay together daydreaming and thinking about what the future would bring, and Tracy said, 'It's dinner time, what shall we have?'

Thomas replied, 'What am I allowed?'

'MMM!' said Tracy, 'how about we have some crisps to start and then some chocolate ice cream with some pop, will that be all right for you?'

'Yes that will be lovely,' and he dashed over and got everything they wanted off the piles of goodies and ate until they were that full they thought they were going to pop. Just as their dinner was settling, they felt the lorry slow down and stop. A few seconds later the engine stopped and the driver's door opened. Quickly they tidied all the rubbish away and Thomas whispered, 'I am going to look outside.' He popped his head under the curtains on the wagon and Tracy heard him shout, 'Yippee!'

She quickly grabbed hold of his ankles and dragged him back inside and said to him sternly, 'You will have to remember to be careful, otherwise you might end up in another jail.'

Thomas knew he had done wrong, but he was so excited he could hardly speak. He started to say, 'But – but – but – funfair, ice cream, beach...'

Tracy put her hand over his mouth and told him to calm down, then she said she would have a look herself, and peeped under the curtain. She saw the sun shining, loads of humans walking around eating all kinds of lovely treats like rock, candyfloss, ice cream, all seaside treats. Behind these people she saw the beach and the sea, with people paddling and children playing on the beach. Tracy thought, *ooh, it looks like the ticklefish are here as well,* for everybody on the beach was laughing uncontrollably. She went back inside and said, 'I can see why you are so excited, and I would love to stay here a while and have some fun, but you must promise to be sensible at least till we find somewhere safe to stay.'

Thomas said he would try his hardest, so they both slid down the piece of string that tied the curtain and ran onto the beach and under one of the piers. When they knew they hadn't been seen, they had a good look round and saw that the pier was made out of huge pieces of wood put deep into the sand so they looked a bit like trees, and then a floor had been put on top with all kinds of rides and seaside things. Thomas said to Tracy, 'Look at that wood that looks like trees, it's got seaweed half way up it. We could climb up to where two pieces of wood are joined together and that would make a good hideout and there is loads of delicious seaweed to eat...'

Tracy thought it was a brilliant idea, because she hadn't told Thomas but she liked seaweed as much as Thomas like nettles and rope and chocolate and just about anything really. They climbed up to their new hideout and sat and ate seaweed and had a good look around, then Tracy noticed that the tide was coming in and asked Thomas what they should do. 'Nothing,' he said, 'we will be very safe here because humans will not come when the tide is in.' They were sitting relaxing and Thomas leaned back against the wood, looked up at the holes in the floor of the pier and he started to chuckle to himself, and Tracy wanted to know why. Thomas pointed up at the holes and said, 'We can have some good fun with those holes, just watch.' He stood up so he was near one of the holes and ROARED like a troll terrier. Everybody near the hole stopped, looked around them, and walked away quickly so Thomas ROARED as loud as he could and little children and mums and even some dads screamed and shouted, 'Run, there's a wild animal around somewhere!' and everybody ran away.

Tracy said, 'We will certainly have some fun here,' and they both really laughed and thought about what they could do next. When all the humans had come back, Tracy said, 'Watch this, it's my turn for fun,' and she waited until somebody walked by with a dog then she meowed like a cat through the hole and watched the dog look around and start barking. They carried on for the rest of the day being mischievous and eating seaweed until it was time for bed.

***

When they woke up in the morning they had their breakfast and decided that they would explore before all the humans got up. The tide had gone out, so they climbed down to the beach and out from under the pier; it was still quite dark and there were different coloured lights hung up everywhere. 'Doesn't it look beautiful,' said Tracy and held Thomas's hand as they walked on the beach. A little later, Tracy said, 'Let's go up to the pavement and see if the humans have left anything that we might find useful for us.'

Thomas climbed into a rubbish bin and he found some cold fish and chips and a bit of candyflossand a piece of soggy ice cream corner. He threw some of each of them out of the bin to Tracy.Then just as he was climbing out, he saw a piece of wire covered in pink plastic, the kind that humans put round sweetie bags. He picked it up and put it in his pocket. When he had climbed down to the pavement, they sat on the beach and packed their food in a piece of newspaper and sat a while looking at all the lights and listening to the birds.

Eventually it started to get to daylight, so they ran onto the pier to see what all the houses were. There were amusements, little shops, a pub. They were that busy looking round that they didn't see a family of humans, and a little boy shouted, 'Look daddy, there's a funny animal, can I have one please?'

Both Thomas and Tracy ran to a hole in the floor and dived through it, not knowing what was on the other side. Luckily for them, the tide was in and they landed in the sea instead of the beach. They swam to the wooden posts and climbed up. Thomas saw a piece of fishing line and tied the pack of food from the bin to it. When they had got to their hideout Thomas pulled up the food and put it out to dry. Then they took their jumpers and shoes and socks off and put them to dry. As they were waiting for their clothes to dry, it started raining then thunder and lightning. Tracy said, 'We can't go out in this, shall we just cuddle up and keep warm?'

Thomas nodded and said he thought it was a good idea. He liked to cuddle with Tracy but sometimes if they got too close the hair from their ears got tangled.The thunder and lightning got louder and Thomas said to Tracy, 'Tracy, if I use one of our wishes and ask freya the Viking goddess of love to come down and hold the service, will you marry me?'

Tracy went all shy and tearful and said, 'I would love to marry you and spend the next two hundred years of my life with you.'

'Oh, thank you, thank you,' Thomas said and gave her a big hug. 'I will cast the spell just as soon as it stops raining.' They sat in their hideout and talked about what they would do and where they would go. Tracy said, 'One day, I would like to go home and have a family but not for fifty or sixty years.'

Thomas agreed and said, 'I might not be in trouble in Troll Town by then.' They were happy, warm and dry, and before they knew it, it was night time so they decided they would try the spell in the morning.

During the night, Tracy heard a scraping and a clicking sound. She had no idea what it was, so she asked Thomas what he thought. He looked around and said he didn't know what it was. Then he heard a splash in the sea and saw a huge crab climbing up the post, clicking its claws coming toward them.

Straightaway, Thomas said, 'Go away, crab, you're not having us for supper!' The crab kept getting nearer and Tracy was frightened so Thomas had a piece of troll toffee, picked up the fishing line he had found, and jumped on the crab's back. The crab tried grabbing him with one of his giant claws, but he only managed to get his braces, which stretched really tight, pulled the fasteners off Thomas's trousers, then sprang back and bashed the crab in the eye. Then while the crab couldn't see properly through his bashed eye, Thomas got the fishing line and tied his claws together, saying that will teach you to mess with Thomas the mighty troll. The crab ran down the post back into the sea, never to be seen again.

In the morning they were that excited they couldn't eat breakfast. Thomas asked Tracy if she still wanted to marry him. She said after the way he protected her from the crab, she wanted to spend the rest of her life married to him. 'Right,' said Thomas, 'I am going ask Freya to come down,' and he chanted... 'Oh, goddess of love from heaven above, come down and marry us, then fly like a dove.' Everything around them became peaceful and pink and white bubbles began to rise out of the sea. And then gentle mist that smelt of roses appeared, and out of the mist came Freya, the Viking goddess of love.

She put a hand on each of their heads and said in a heavenly voice, 'Hello, my little trolls. I understand you would like me to marry you.'

Both Tracy and Thomas were speechless by the sight of such a beautiful heavenly goddess, and all they could do was nod. Freya told them, 'It is a great pleasure to marry you, but first you must tell me why you are not in your homeland of Norway.' So they both told Freya what they had done, and she said to them, 'Would you like me to marry you and make a spell that you can go back to Norway in five years?'

Tracy said, 'Yes please, that would be lovely wouldn't it.'

Thomas agreed and said, 'Will I be forgiven by then?'

Freya said if you both swear that you love Norway and everything that lives and grows there, you will be forgiven in five years. Freya performed the wedding and cast the spell, blew them both a kiss, and said, 'You are married now.' Then she turned into a dove and flew away. Thomas and Tracy looked at each other and gave each other a kiss on the lips. Then all of the bubbles that had come out of the sea popped, and there were elves flying around and a wedding cake and all different kinds of food appeared, but to Thomas and Tracy's surprise, Ronnie had arrived. He dashed over to Thomas and Tracy and they all hugged each other and all three of them were talking at the same time and laughing with each other. It got very noisy and happy.

Thomas said, 'Ronnie, I never thought I would see you again, are you still on Captain Willy Welks' ship? Does he still chase pirates? What happened to Captain Jellybelly?'

Ronnie said, 'Just a minute, calm down! First of all, congratulations to you both on getting married. Now, I think you should make a speech, and then we can have some food and you two can cut the cake.'

Thomas gulped. 'Me, a speech? I have never done that before, I don't know what to say.'

'You just thank everybody for coming and tell them to enjoy themselves.'

'Must I?' Thomas said. Ronnie just nodded. Thomas stood up and said, 'Excuse me please, everybody.' Everything went quiet and Thomas said softly, 'Thank you all for coming, please eat what you want and enjoy yourselves,' then he sat down very quickly.

Ronnie smiled and patted him on the shoulder and said, 'Let's get some food and then the three of us should talk.'

They got their food and talked until it was time to cut the cake, and after they had eaten the cake it was getting very late, and the elves were getting tired and started to leave until Ronnie was the only one left. When he said it was time to go, Tracy said to him, 'Must you go? Please stay for the night, there is room for you here and we still have so much to talk about.'

Ronnie agreed and all three of them snuggled up in the hideout and slept until morning came. When morning came, none of them were hungry so they went for a nice long walk on the beach before it got busy and talked about what they had done and what they would like to do in the future. Ronnie said when he left them he was going back to sea, only this he was thinking of going on a cruise ship, because they went to nice places and there was always loads of food. 'Why don't you come with me?' he asked them both.

'No,' said Thomas, 'I am a married troll now,' giving Tracy a squeeze. 'I will have to start to learn to behave, you never know, I might be a daddy in the next fifty years.'

'What have you got planned then?'

'I don't really know, have you any ideas Tracy?' Thomas said.

'I would like to go nearer to Norway,' she said. 'Freya did say we could go back there in five years' time. What about going to the highlands of Scotland and see if it's nice there?'

'That sounds a long long way away,' Thomas replied. 'I think it would take forever,but if we set off today and try to get on lorries we might get there one day.'

Ronnie said to them, 'Just a minute, I haven't got you a wedding present yet, how about if I did a honeymoon spell for you?'

Tracy said, 'That sounds nice, what is it?'

'Well, the humans have a thing called a drainage system, it's pipes underground where the rainwater goes so their houses don't get flooded. I will make a spell so that you have a speed boat in the pipes that will take you to the highlands of Scotland in a day. You will be travelling that fast that nothing will get in your way.'

Thomas and Tracy jumped up and down with joy and waved their arms in the air shouting, 'Hooray, thank you Ronnie, thank you!'

Ronnie made the spell and said goodbye to them both, and before he went he said, 'You never know, we might meet again one day.'

After they had climbed down into the boat, they got settled into the seats and fastened the safety belts. Thomas pressed the start button and the boat started to move; it went faster and faster until their hair was blowing in the wind. They were screaming and shouting and really having fun and they could see anything that was in the pipes running out of the way... Except for one. It was a big rat! It was about as big as terrier troll dog, and it stood in front of the boat, hoping they would stop, but Thomas just sprayed it with spray that smells horrible and the rat pulled a funny face and ran away. They laughed at the face the rat pulled, and said he looked as if he had pulled his face inside out. Before they knew it, they were in Scotland.

They climbed out of the boat and up to the cover that is on the drain to stop anything falling down it. They peeped out and saw a few humans walking around, but there were only a few houses and not many cars. Some of the men were wearing kilts and a furry purse that is called a sporran. They both thought it was safe enough to climb out and run under a wooden shed that was near. After they got under the shed, they looked out and in the distance they saw big hills and mountains with snow on. Tracy sighed and said, 'Isn't it beautiful? It looks a lot like Norway. I hope it is as nice when we get there.'

'Well, we will find out in the next day or so. Shall we set off now and get something to eat on the way?'

'Yes please,' said Tracy. 'I can't wait till we get there, it does look lovely.'

They sneaked out of the village without being seen and into the countryside. It was peaceful; all they could hear were birds singing and lambs baaing. As they walked along without a care in the world, looking for a nice place to have dinner, they heard a stream gurgling not far away and went to have a look. It didn't take long to find it and it looked beautiful. Birds were eating, little fish were swimming. Tracy saw that some of them were ticklefish, and said to Thomas, 'I wonder where they are going.' There were mice and spiders and every animal was friendly towards one another. When they got to the bank of the stream, Thomas saw a big patch of wild watercress growing and took his shoes and socks off, paddled into the stream, and had a taste of the cress. It was crunchy and tasted lovely, so he pulled enough for himself and Tracy. They sat by the stream and ate the cress and dranksome of the cold crystal clear water, then they lay on their backs looking at the blue sky and fluffy white clouds.

Tracy said she thought they should build a place to stay for the night, then just spend the rest of the lazing about and carry on in the morning.

In the morning, they were up nice and early, had a wash in the stream then they had some more cress for breakfast and collected dew off the grass to drink and after a good night's sleep and full tummies they set off toward the highlands. They didn't rush because they felt safe and kept looking for somewhere they could call home. As they got to the bottom of a mountain, they heard a noise that sounded like a donkey. They looked at each other and said, 'We must go and see what that is.' As they went towards the noise, they saw a donkey and it was trotting round and saying 'heehaw, heehaw' and then they saw four ticklefish tickling its tummy and realised it was laughing and trying to get away but couldn't.

'This looks such a happy place,' Tracy said, 'let's have a look around.'

'All right,' said Thomas, and both of them turned around and a great big human lady was stood looking down at them.

Both Thomas and Tracy froze with fright and the lady said, 'Hahaaa! What have we here... are you trolls from Norway? You needn't be frightened of me, I have met trolls before.'

Thomas thought, *I had better say something or she will think we are rude*, so he told her their names and that they had just got married and were looking for somewhere to live.

'Well, my name is Chrissy MacCarr but please call me Chrissy, and if you want somewhere to live there is a nice little cave just over there at the bottom of the steep hill. It used belong to a troll called Tyson, but he went back to Norway, did you know him?'

'No,' Thomas said. 'Can we please go and look at the cave?'

'Of course you can, and I hope you like it because I am on my own up here and if you stay I will have somebody to talk to.'

Tracy and Thomas went to the cave and when they went inside it had furniture in it; there were tables, chairs, beds, wardrobes, carpets, everything that was needed was there.

'Can we stay, Thomas, please can we stay? It is so much like home, the house, the countryside, the weather, everything.'

'I am glad you like it because I want to stay as well Shall we go tell Chrissy?'

As they were running back to tell Chrissy, they heard donkeys all over the place. They stopped to have a look and there must have been twenty donkeys, all being tickled by ticklefish. They were all saying 'heehaw, heehaw' and running round and having fun. When they saw Chrissy, they told her they were stopping, and thanked her. And then Thomas asked why there so many donkeys about.

'Didn't you know this is a donkey sanctuary? All the donkeys that get too old to give rides to children on a beach come here to retire, and I look after them.'

'Could we please help?' Tracy asked. 'I bet it is great fun.'

'It can be hard work sometimes,' Chrissy said. 'The amount of times I have had to go up that steep hill to help them down when they get stuck, I think my legs are getting shorter. I am eighty years old you know, and for a human to be climbing hills that is old.'

'We could go up that hill really quickly and help them, we are only sixty years old and for troll that is young.'

'If you promise not to tease donkeys or be nasty to them, I would love you to help me and perhaps we could be friends. Will you help starting tomorrow?' Chrissy asked them.

Both Thomas and Tracy went back to their new house Thomas gave Tracy a kiss and said, 'I think it will be nice here until our next adventure.'

The End